DIANE GOODE'S
BOOK OF
Giants
& little people

Dutton Children's Books

NEW YORK

FOR PETER

ACKNOWLEDGMENTS

"How Big-Mouth Wrestled the Giant." From *Three Giant Stories* by Lesley Conger. Text copyright © 1968 by Lesley Conger. Reprinted by permission of Simon & Schuster Books for Young Readers, an imprint of Simon & Schuster Children's Publishing Division.

"The Little Men," by Flora Fearne. Reprinted by permission of HarperCollins Publishers Limited.

"Three Strong Women." From *Three Strong Women* by Claus Stamm. Copyright © 1962 by Claus Stamm and Kazue Mizumura. Reprinted by permission of Viking Penguin, a division of Penguin Books USA Inc.

"I want my breakfast," by Eve Merriam. From *Blackberry Ink* by Eve Merriam. Copyright © 1985 by Eve Merriam. Reprinted by permission of Marian Reiner.

"Anansi and the Plantains," originally entitled "Anansi and the Magic Pot," from *Tales from West Indian Folklore, retold for English Children* by Lucille Iremonger. Copyright © 1956 by Lucille Iremonger. Published by George G. Harrap & Co. Ltd.

"A Fairy Went A-Marketing," by Rose Fyleman. From *Fairies and Chimneys* by Rose Fyleman. Reprinted by permission of The Society of Authors as the literary representative of the Estate of Rose Fyleman.

"Lovesick Lopez," originally entitled "Old Sock and the Swimming Pigs," from *American Tall-Tale Animals* by Adrien Stoutenburg. Copyright © 1968 by Adrien Stoutenburg. First appeared in *Tall Tale Animals*, published by The Viking Press. Reprinted by permission of Curtis Brown, Ltd.

"Little Lella," retold by Donna Jo Napoli. Copyright © 1996 Donna Jo Napoli.

"Teeny Tiny Ghost," by Lilian Moore. From *Spooky Rhymes and Riddles* by Lilian Moore. Copyright © 1972 by Lilian Moore. Reprinted by permission of Scholastic Inc.

"Magic Story for Falling Asleep," by Nancy Willard. Copyright © 1976 by Nancy Willard. Reprinted from *Giant Poems*, published by Holiday House, by permission of the author.

Library of Congress Cataloging-in-Publication Data

Diane Goode's book of giants & little people.—1st ed. p. cm.
Summary: Tales, nursery rhymes, and poems featuring characters that are
extraordinarily large or small, such as giants, elves, and fairies.
ISBN 0-525-45660-0
[1. Giants—Literary collections. 2. Fairies—Literary collections.
3. Size—Literary collections.] I. Goode, Diane.
PZ5.D52 1997
398.21—dc21 97-6991 CIP AC

Selections collected and adapted by Lucia Monfried
Copyright © 1997 by Diane Goode · All rights reserved
Published in the United States 1997 by Dutton Children's Books, a division of
Penguin Books USA Inc., 375 Hudson Street, New York, New York 10014
Designed by Sara Reynolds · Printed in Hong Kong
First Edition
1 3 5 7 9 10 8 6 4 2

contents

introduction

M Y MOTHER, WHO WAS A MARVELOUS STORYTELLER, ALWAYS said, "If you want to tell a good story, you have to exaggerate things." I believe she was right.

Folktales were, and still are, my favorite stories. They were the most exciting and the most satisfying. Ordinary characters could, by wit and courage, control their own fates. There was no confusion between right and wrong, and those in the right always won. Anything was possible in these tales, and best of all, things were exaggerated in the extreme. Little people were very, very little, and big people were giants.

The lives of the people who created these stories were very different from ours. A person then might have felt very small in the face of enemies, both real and imagined, and enemies could be exaggerated into veritable giants. It required bravery and ingenuity to survive, with a touch of humor too. Giant characters could help explain things not understood from the natural world, just as tiny elves and fairies could be thought to assist one and perhaps bring good fortune. With the help of tales, the impossible becomes possible.

Of course, not all giants were enemies; some were good, and some were just dim-witted. Not all little people were helpful, like the shoemaker's elves. There were bad fairies, evil sprites, and nasty imps.

Children face many challenges today, though different from those of our forefathers. They may feel very small in a world of giants. I think of these tales as magic mirrors. True, they exaggerate the image. But they also reflect back to us a belief in the goodness of our fellow man and show that an ordinary person has the power within to become a superhero, and conquer his or her world. The image is a powerful and positive one…and that's no exaggeration.

Fay Folks

a brownie child,
    A dwarf, a sprite
Can dance in print
    On pages white.

A goblin, giant,
    Troll, or gnome
Can claim a book
    To be his home.

A fairy queen,
    A woodland elf
Can live in books
    Upon the shelf.

Anonymous

how big-mouth wrestled the giant

TRADITIONAL

THERE WAS ONCE A LAD KNOWN FOR his bragging. Everyone called him Big-Mouth.

Whenever that braggart, Big-Mouth, told about anything he saw, it became the biggest, or the ugliest, or the best, ever. And Big-Mouth himself was the bravest, smartest young man in the whole countryside—according to Big-Mouth. But, of course, no one believed him at all.

Big-Mouth was always bragging about how he would fight the giant who lived in the Wood and make him cry for mercy. "I'll send him running for cover," he said. "Wait and see!"

One day it happened that Big-Mouth had to go through the wood. As he walked, Big-Mouth talked to himself, for his tongue was never still.

"If I meet that giant," he said, "I'll wrestle him and win, I will."

"HALT!" cried the giant, suddenly appearing in front of the lad.

Big-Mouth took one look at who had spoken and jumped into the pile of uprooted trees that the giant had just flung by the side of the path.

"Oh, afraid, are you?" roared the giant.

"Afraid?" cried Big-Mouth. "I should say not! I'm—I'm—I'm just hunting for the biggest tree to hit you with!"

The giant blinked his eyes. What kind of fellow was this, anyway?

He reached in and dragged Big-Mouth out into the open by his shirttail.

"Let's wrestle!" bellowed the giant.

Poor Big-Mouth! Struggling in the giant's grasp, he began to sweat. His eyes bulged, and his teeth chattered with fright. He opened his mouth. "You—you'd better watch out, you!" he said.

"Watch out?" roared the giant. "Why, look at you—you're so scared, you're covered with sweat! Any minute you'll be begging for mercy!"

There was nothing Big-Mouth wanted more than mercy. But, alas, his bragging tongue just wouldn't say the word.

"I'm—I'm not sweating," he said. "I'm g-g-greasing myself—so you won't be able to hang on to me!"

The giant almost lost him at that, for he was slippery. "Well then," snarled the giant, tightening his grip, "why are your eyes bulging like that? Any minute now you'll beg me to let go so you can breathe again!"

"Oh no, I won't!" squeaked Big-Mouth with what little breath he had. "My eyes are bulging because I'm—I'm looking around for a g-g-good p-p-place to throw you!"

This was almost too much. With a bellow of rage, the giant held Big-Mouth up right in front of his ugly face.

"Well, in that case," he roared, "tell me why your teeth are chattering. Just tell me that!"

With such a close view of the giant's teeth, poor Big-Mouth nearly fainted dead away. But not even that could stop his bragging tongue.

"M-my teeth aren't ch-chattering!" he cried. "I'm—I'm sh-sh-sharpening them to b-bite off your n-n-n-nose!"

And at that, the giant clapped his hand over his nose, dropped Big-Mouth to the ground, and ran away deep into the woods. He was never heard from again.

But in case you think this shows that bragging is a good idea, let me tell you the rest.

When Big-Mouth returned home, nobody believed him—not even his brother, although he was kind enough to tell me the story.

the shoemaker and the elves

TRADITIONAL

THERE WAS ONCE A SHOEMAKER WHO worked very hard, but he could not earn enough to live on. At last all he had in the world was gone, except enough leather to make one pair of shoes. He cut out the shoes to make up the next day and then went to bed.

In the morning, he sat down to work, but there, to his great wonder, stood the shoes, already made and as beautiful as could be. The shoemaker didn't know what to think.

That day a customer came in and paid a high price for the shoes. The poor shoemaker bought enough leather to make two more pairs. In the evening, he cut out the work and went to bed. When he got up in the morning, he saw that the work was finished.

More buyers came in, and they, too, paid him well for his shoes. So he bought enough leather for four pairs.

Again he cut out the work at night and found it finished in the morning. So it went for some time. And the man became prosperous again.

One evening he said to his wife, "I want to stay up and watch who comes and does my work for me." The wife agreed, so they hid behind a curtain and watched to see what would happen.

At midnight, two little naked elves sat down at the shoemaker's bench and began to work, quickly stitching and rapping and tapping away.

When they were finished, they ran off, as quick as lightning.

The next day his wife said to the shoemaker, "These little elves have made us rich, and we ought to do them a good deed in return. They must be cold, running about with nothing on. I will make each of them a shirt, a coat, a vest, and a pair of

pants. You make each of them a little pair of shoes." The good shoemaker agreed.

When all the things were ready, he and his wife laid them on the table. Then they went and hid behind the curtain.

At midnight, the elves came in and were about to sit down to their work as usual when they saw the clothes lying there. They laughed in surprise and delight. They dressed themselves in the twinkling of an eye, then danced around the room and out the door.

The shoemaker never saw them again, but everything went well with him from that time forward.

the little men

Would you see the little men
Coming down a moonlit glen?—
Gnome and elf and woodland sprite,
Clad in brown and green and white,
Skipping, hopping, never stopping,
Stumbling, grumbling, tumbling, mumbling,
Dancing, prancing, singing, swinging—
Coats of red and coats of brown,
Put on straight or upside down,
Outside in or inside out,
Some with sleeves and some without,
Rustling, bustling, stomping, romping,
Strumming, humming, hear them coming—
You will see the Little Men
If it be a Fairy glen.

Flora Fearne

three strong women

JAPANESE

LONG AGO, IN JAPAN, THERE LIVED A famous wrestler with legs as big as trees. He was on his way to the capital to wrestle before the Emperor.

He strode down the road feeling much as a wrestler should—strong, healthy, and rather conceited.

They call me Forever-Mountain, he thought, because I am such a good, strong wrestler—big, too. I'm a fine, brave man and far too modest ever to say so....

Just then he saw a round girl with red cheeks and a nose like a button.

"If I don't tickle that girl, I shall regret it all my life," said the wrestler under his breath. So he tiptoed up and poked her lightly in the ribs with one huge finger.

The girl giggled and brought one arm down so that the wrestler's hand was caught between it and her body.

"Ho-ho-ho! You've caught me! I can't move at all!" said the wrestler, laughing.

"I know," said the jolly girl.

He started to pull his hand free, but somehow he could not.

"Now, now—let me go, little girl," he said. "I am a very powerful man. If I pull too hard, I might hurt you."

"Pull," said the girl. "I admire powerful men."

She began to walk, and though the wrestler tugged and pulled until his feet dug great furrows in the ground, he had to follow.

"Please let me go," he pleaded. "I am the famous wrestler Forever-

Mountain. I must wrestle before the Emperor"—he burst out weeping—"and you're hurting my hand!"

"You poor, sweet little Forever-Mountain," she said. "Are you tired? Shall I carry you?"

"No! I do not want you to carry me. I want you to let me go," moaned the pitiful wrestler.

"I only want to help you," said the girl, now pulling him up a mountain path. "Oh, I am sure you'll have no trouble with the other wrestlers. But what if you meet a really *strong* man someday? Come along to my mother's house," she continued, "and we'll make a strong man of you. The wrestling in the capital is three months away."

"All right. I'll come along," said the wrestler, who saw he had no choice.

Soon they arrived in a small valley. A simple farmhouse with a thatched roof stood in the middle.

"Grandmother is at home, but she is an old lady, and she's probably sleeping. But Mother should be bringing our cow back from the field—oh, there's Mother now!"

She waved. The woman coming around the corner of the house put down the cow she had been carrying and came across the grass.

"These mountain paths are full of stones. They hurt the cow's feet. And who is the nice young man you've brought, Maru-me?"

The girl, whose name was Maru-me, explained everything. "And we have only three months!" she finished.

"Well, it's not very long, and he does look terribly feeble. Maybe when he gets stronger, he can help Grandmother with some of the easy work about the house."

"Fine!" said the girl, and she called her grandmother.

"I'm coming!" came a creaky voice from inside the house, and a little old woman tottered out the door. As she came toward them, she stumbled over the roots of a great oak tree.

"Heh! My eyes aren't what they used to be," she complained, wrapping her skinny arms around its trunk and pulling it out of the ground.

Then she picked up the tree and threw it away. It landed with a faint crash far up the mountainside.

"Ah, how clumsy," she said. "I meant to throw it *over* the mountain."

The wrestler was not listening. He had quietly fainted.

"Oh! We must put him to bed," said Maru-me.

"Here, let me carry him, he's light," said the grandmother. She slung him over her shoulder and carried him into the house.

The next day, they began the work of making Forever-Mountain over into what they thought a strong man should be. They gave him food meant to toughen him. Every day he was made to do the work of five men, and every evening he wrestled with Grandmother, because she was the least likely to injure him accidentally.

He grew stronger and stronger, but Grandmother could still throw him easily into the air—and catch him again.

His legs had been like logs; now they were like pillars. His big hands were hard as stones, and when he cracked his knuckles, the sound was like trees splitting on a cold night.

One evening, near the end of his third month, he wrestled with Grandmother and held her down for half a minute.

Maru-me squealed with joy and threw her arms around him.

They agreed that he was now ready to show some *real* strength before the Emperor.

"But I will return," said Forever-Mountain. "Then I will ask your mother's and grandmother's permission to marry you. I want to be one of the family."

Next morning, Forever-Mountain thanked Maru-me and her mother and grandmother, and trudged up the mountain.

When he reached the palace grounds, many of the other wrestlers were already there, sitting about, eating enormous bowls of rice, comparing one another's weight, and telling stories.

The Emperor and all the ladies and gentlemen of the court were waiting for the wrestling to begin.

The first two wrestlers chosen to fight were Forever-Mountain and a wrestler who was said to have the biggest stomach in the country. He raised his foot and brought it down with a fearful stamp. Then he glared fiercely at Forever-Mountain.

Forever-Mountain raised his foot. He brought it down.

There was a sound like thunder, the earth shook, and the other wrestler bounced into the air and out of the ring, as gracefully as a soap bubble.

He picked himself up and bowed to the Emperor.

"I do not think I shall wrestle this season," he said. And he walked out.

Five other wrestlers then and there decided that they were not wrestling this season, either.

From then on, Forever-Mountain brought his foot down lightly with each new wrestler, then he picked him up very gently, carried him out, and placed him before the Emperor, bowing every time.

The Emperor awarded all the prize money to Forever-Mountain.

"But," he said, "you had better not wrestle anymore." He waggled his finger at the other wrestlers, who were sitting on the ground, weeping like great fat babies.

Forever-Mountain promised, and everybody looked relieved. "I think I shall become a farmer," he said, and left at once to go back to Maru-me.

Maru-me was waiting for him. When she saw him coming, she ran down the mountain, picked him up, together with the heavy bags of prize money, and carried him halfway up the mountainside. Then she giggled and put him down. The rest of the way she let him carry her.

Forever-Mountain married Maru-me and never fought in public again. But up in the mountains, sometimes, the earth shakes and rumbles, and they say that is Forever-Mountain and Maru-me's grandmother practicing wrestling in the hidden valley.

"I want my breakfast"

"I want my breakfast,"
The giant said,
"The minute that I wake up
In my giant bed.

"Tell the kitchen,"
The giant said,
"I'm giantly hungry,
And I better get fed.

"I don't want oatmeal
Or eggs with toast.
I want what I want
And I want it the most.

"One hundred pancakes
And not one less,
And enough maple syrup
To make a giant mess."

Eve Merriam

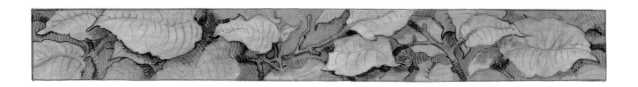

anansi
and the
plantains

WEST INDIAN

IT WAS MARKET DAY, BUT ANANSI HAD no money. He sat at the door of his cottage and watched all the others hurrying to the market to buy and sell. He had nothing to sell, for he had not done any work in his field. How was he to find food for his wife and for the children? Above all, how was he to find food for himself?

Soon his wife came to the door and spoke to him. "You must go and find something for us to eat. What are we going to do without a scrap of food in the house?"

"I am going out to work for some food," said Anansi. "You just watch and see!"

Anansi walked about until noon and found nothing, so he lay down and slept in the shade of a mango tree all afternoon. Then, in the cool of the evening, he set off for home. He walked slowly, for he was ashamed to be going home empty-handed. He was asking himself what he was to do when he met his old friend Rat going home with a large bunch of plantains on his head.

Anansi's eyes shone when he saw the plantains, and he stopped to speak to his friend Rat.

"How are you, my friend Rat? I haven't seen you for a very long time."

"Oh, I am staggering along, staggering along," said Rat. "And how are you—and the family?"

Anansi put on his longest face. "Ah, Brother Rat," he groaned, "times are hard, very hard. I can hardly find a thing to eat from one day to the next." At this, tears came into his eyes, and he went on:

"I walked all yesterday. I have been walking all today, and I haven't found a yam or a plantain." He glanced at the large bunch of plantains. "Ah, Brother Rat, the children will have nothing but water for supper tonight."

"I am sorry to hear that," said Rat, "very sorry indeed. I know how I would feel if I had to go home to my wife and children without any food."

"Without even a plantain," said Anansi, and again he looked at the plantains on Rat's head.

Brother Rat put the plantains on the ground and looked at them, too.

At last Anansi spoke. "My friend," he said, "what a lovely bunch of plantains! Where did you get it in these hard times?"

"It's all that I had left in my field, Anansi. This bunch must last until the peas are ready."

"They will be ready soon. Brother Rat," Anansi pleaded, "give me one or two of the plantains. The children have eaten nothing, and they have only water for supper."

"Well . . . perhaps, Brother Anansi, perhaps!" said Rat. He counted all the plantains carefully and then said, "All right." Then he counted them again, broke off the four smallest plantains, and gave them to Anansi.

"Thank you," said Anansi, "thank you, my good friend. But Rat, you have given me only four plantains, and there are five of us in the family—my wife, the three children, and myself."

Rat took no notice of this. He only said, "Help me to put this bunch of plantains on my head, Brother Anansi, and do not try to break off any more."

So Anansi had to help Rat put the bunch of plantains back on his head. Then Anansi set off for his home. He walked quickly, because the four plantains were not a heavy burden. When he got home, he handed the four plantains to his wife and told her to roast them. Then he went outside and sat down in the shade of a mango tree until his wife called out to say that the plantains were ready.

Anansi went back inside. There were the four plantains, nicely roasted.

He took up one and gave it to his girl. He gave one each to the two boys. He gave the last and biggest plantain to his wife. After that he sat down empty-handed and very, very sad-looking. His wife said to him, "Don't you want some of the plantains?"

"No," said Anansi, with a deep sigh. "There are only enough for four of us. It's better for me to remain hungry as long as your stomachs are filled."

"No, Papa," shouted the children, "you must have half of my plantain." They all broke their plantains in two, and each one gave Anansi a half. When his wife saw what was happening, she gave Anansi half of her plantain, too. So, in the end, Anansi got more than anyone, just as usual.

a fairy went a-marketing

A fairy went a-marketing—
She bought a little fish;
She put it in a crystal bowl
Upon a golden dish.
An hour she sat in wonderment
And watched its silver gleam,
And then she gently took it up
And slipped it in a stream.

A fairy went a-marketing—
She bought a colored bird;
It sang the sweetest, shrillest song
That ever she had heard.
She sat beside its painted cage
And listened half the day,
And then she opened wide the door
And let it fly away.

A fairy went a-marketing—
She bought a winter gown
All stitched about with gossamer
And lined with thistledown.
She wore it all the afternoon
With prancing and delight,
Then gave it to a little frog
To keep him warm at night.

A fairy went a-marketing—
She bought a gentle mouse
To take her tiny messages,
To keep her tiny house.
All day she kept its busy feet
Pit-patting to and fro,
And then she kissed its silken ears,
Thanked it, and let it go.

Rose Fyleman

managing molly

ENGLISH

THERE WAS ONCE AN OGRE AS GREEDY AS he was rich. The more he had, the more he wanted, and no one had ever gotten the better of him.

This Ogre had to keep getting married, because his wives always died soon after the wedding. So he was constantly courting fresh ones. When choosing a new wife, the Ogre cared only for one thing—he wanted her to be a good and thrifty housekeeper.

There was such a woman in the village. Managing Molly, as she was called, was the daughter of a very poor farmer. Since he could not afford a dowry for her, she had never married. Everyone figured that she should marry the Ogre.

Sure enough, the Ogre came to the farm and invited himself to supper for the following week.

Managing Molly was not worried.

"Do what I bid you, and say as I say," she said to her father, "and if the Ogre does not change his mind, you won't come out of it empty-handed."

Following his daughter's wishes, the farmer used all his money and

bought a great number of hares and a barrel of white wine. Molly borrowed new linens from her neighbors and filled the kitchen shelves. On the day of the Ogre's visit, she prepared a delicious stew with the hares and set the wine barrel out.

When the Ogre came, Molly served up the stew, and the Ogre sat down to sup. The stew was perfect. The Ogre was very pleased and said politely, "I'm afraid, my dear, that you have been put to great trouble and expense on my account."

"Don't mention it, sir," said Molly. "The fewer rats, the more corn. How do *you* cook rats?"

"Not one of all the extravagant hussies I have had as wives ever cooked them at all," said the Ogre, and he thought to himself: "Such a stew, and of rats! What thrift! What a housewife!"

"I suppose you spin?" he inquired.

Molly held out a linen towel for him to see. "All that came off my wheel."

But as her hand was raised toward the shelves, the Ogre thought that all the linen he saw there was from thread of her spinning, and his admiration grew even more.

When he tasted the wine, he was still more pleased, for it was the best. "This must have cost you a great deal, neighbor," said the Ogre, drinking to the farmer's health as Molly left the room.

"It's the best way to use up rotten apples," said the farmer. "But I leave all that to Molly."

"We give our rotten apples to the pigs," growled the Ogre. "But things will improve when she is my wife."

The Ogre was now in a great hurry to conclude the match and asked what dowry the farmer would give his daughter.

"I should never dream of giving a dowry with Molly. Whoever gets her gets dowry enough. On the contrary, I shall expect a good sum from the man who takes her from me."

The Ogre was anxious to secure this thrifty bride at any price. He named a large sum of money, thinking, "We shall live on rats from now on, and the money saved will soon pay for the dowry."

"Double that, and we'll see," said the farmer stoutly.

So the Ogre named a sum that the farmer agreed to that was enough to make the farmer rich for life.

"Bring it in a sack tomorrow morning," he said, "and then you can speak to Molly. She's gone to bed now."

The next morning, the Ogre appeared, carrying the dowry money in a sack. Molly came to meet him.

"There are two things," she said, "I would ask of any husband: a new farmhouse, built as I should direct, and a featherbed of fresh goose feathers, filled when the old woman plucks her geese. If I don't sleep well, I cannot work well."

"That's not much," thought the Ogre. "And after all, the house will be my own." So he built it himself, under Molly's orders. He worked hard, day after day. When winter came, it was finished, and a stout house it was.

"Now for the featherbed," said Molly. "I'll make the ticking, and when the old woman plucks her geese, I'll send for you."

When it snows, they say the old woman up yonder is plucking geese. So at the first snowstorm, Molly sent for the Ogre.

"Now the feathers are falling," she said, "so fill up the bed."

"How am I to catch them?" cried the Ogre.

"Stupid! Don't you see them lying all around?" cried Molly. "Get a shovel and set to work."

So the Ogre did. He carried in shovelfuls of snow to the bed. But it melted as fast as he put it in, so his work never seemed done. By nightfall the room was so cold that the snow would not melt, and the featherbed was finally filled.

Molly hastily covered it with sheets and blankets, and said, "Pray rest here tonight, and tell me if the bed is not comfort itself. Tomorrow we will be married."

The tired Ogre lay down on the bed he had filled, but he could not get warm.

"The sheets must be damp," he said, and in the morning he woke with such horrible pains in his bones that he could hardly move. "It's no use," he groaned. "She's a very managing woman, but to sleep on such a bed would be the death of me." And he went home as quickly as he could, before Managing Molly could call upon him to be married.

When Molly found that he had gone, she sent the farmer after him.

"What do you want?" cried the Ogre.

"The bride is waiting for you," said the farmer.

"I'm too ill to be married," said the Ogre.

"She wants to know what you will give her to make up for the disappointment."

"She's got the dowry, and the farm, and the featherbed," groaned the Ogre. "What more is there she could possibly want?"

The farmer soon returned.

"She says you've pressed the featherbed flat, and she wants some more goose feathers."

"Take the geese from my yard, and begone!" yelled the Ogre.

The farmer lost no time in leaving, and he drove home as fine a flock of geese as you will ever see.

It is said that the Ogre never recovered from the effects of sleeping on the old woman's feathers. As for Managing Molly, with her good dowry, she was able to pick precisely whom she wanted to marry.

teeny-tiny

ONCE UPON A TIME THERE WAS A teeny-tiny woman who lived in a teeny-tiny house in a teeny-tiny village. Now, one day this teeny-tiny woman put on her teeny-tiny bonnet and went out of her teeny-tiny house to take a teeny-tiny walk. And when this teeny-tiny woman had gone a teeny-tiny way, she came to a teeny-tiny

gate; so the teeny-tiny woman opened the teeny-tiny gate and went into a teeny-tiny churchyard. And when this teeny-tiny woman had got into the teeny-tiny churchyard, she saw a teeny-tiny bone on a teeny-tiny grave. The teeny-tiny woman

said to her teeny-tiny self, "This teeny-tiny bone will make me some teeny-tiny soup for my teeny-tiny supper." So the teeny-tiny woman put the teeny-tiny bone into her teeny-tiny pocket and went home to her teeny-tiny house.

Now, when the teeny-tiny woman got home to her teeny-tiny house, she was a teeny-tiny bit tired; so she went up her teeny-tiny stairs to her teeny-tiny bed and put the teeny-tiny bone into a teeny-tiny cupboard. And when this teeny-tiny woman had been to sleep a teeny-tiny time, she was awakened by a teeny-tiny voice from the teeny-tiny cupboard, which said: "Give me my bone!"

And this teeny-tiny woman was a teeny-tiny frightened, so she hid her teeny-tiny head under the teeny-tiny covers and went to sleep again. And when she had been to sleep again a teeny-tiny time, the teeny-tiny voice again cried out from the teeny-tiny cupboard a teeny-tiny louder: "G I V E M E M Y B O N E !"

This made the teeny-tiny woman a teeny-tiny more frightened, so she hid her teeny-tiny head a teeny-tiny further under the teeny-tiny covers.

And when the teeny-tiny woman had been to sleep again a teeny-tiny time, the teeny-tiny voice from the teeny-tiny cupboard said again, a teeny-tiny louder, "G I V E M E M Y B O N E !"

And this teeny-tiny woman was a teeny-tiny bit more frightened, but she put her teeny-tiny head out of the teeny-tiny covers and said in her loudest teeny-tiny voice, "TAKE IT!"

lovesick lopez

AMERICAN TALL TALE

THE GREAT DON JOSÉ LOPEZ WAS A man with a big heart who did marvelous deeds with his faithful *caballeros* in what is now California.

One day, a Spanish ship arrived with a boar and several sows at the harbor near Lopez's *rancho*. Don José decided that it would be a fine idea to raise pigs for food for his *caballeros*. So he bought the pigs and started raising them. In no time at all he had dozens of pigs and piglets, so fat and healthy and happy that it made the Great Don Lopez's heart and mustache glow just to look at them. When it was time for the butcher to turn the lovely pigs into pork chops, ham, and bacon, Lopez mounted his flying palm tree and flew around for hours, struggling with his conscience. Finally, he rode the tree down to

earth, pushed its roots back into the soil, and told his faithful men that it was impossible to let even one pig be made into sausage. Killing, he said, would be against the whole spirit of his *caballeros*.

Still, food was needed. Don José thought some more and found a solution. The pigs, he declared, should be used for their milk. He trained a group of his men to do the job. So far as is known, they were the first to milk pigs, drink pig's milk, and make pig cheese.

There was one thing that Don José overlooked. Trusting his pigs as he did, he did not built any fences around his *rancho*, so the pigs wandered off the home range and into the garden of a nearby mission built by Spanish *padres*. The pigs nibbled and gnawed and uprooted everything in the priests' garden. This upset the *padres* so terribly that they sent one of their workers to go hunt down the pigs. Don José was heartbroken when he heard the tragic news and decided to teach the *padres* a lesson. Late one night, his *caballeros* crept up to the mission and took the bell that the *padres* used to call the people to worship. They carted the bell to the ranch, hung it high, and rang it at milking time. The pigs soon grew used to the bell's clang and bong, and the moment they heard it they would stampede toward the stable to be milked. No matter how far away they were, they would come rushing to the spot, squealing with love and joy.

This went on and on, and each year, many more piglets were born. Even the Great Don José Lopez, for all that he adored the pigs, realized that something would have to be done. He and his faithful *caballeros* talked the matter over and decided that they would be forced to part with some of their beloved porkers. Everyone was deeply sad and all wept bitter tears.

So they set out on their fine, prancing horses to round up the pigs. When they had coaxed them into a drove, they began herding them to town, where they hoped to find a kind buyer. The pigs went squeaking and squealing onward happily, thinking they were in a parade.

The Great Don Lopez and his order of *caballeros* and all the grunting pigs came into town and were passing the mission when the mission bell started to ring. Everybody stopped in astonishment, including the pigs. The bell tower had been silent all this time. Now a new bell hung in the stolen bell's place, even louder and clearer than the one before. It went BONG! and DING! and DONG!, calling everyone to Mass.

The pigs pricked up their ears and uncurled their tails. They stared at the mission. Then every one of them started charging toward the church, believing it was milking time!

They churned and charged and stampeded into the chapel, where people were already kneeling in the pews. The worshipers gathered by the church went running for safety, thinking that a horde of demons was upon them. The fastest runners raced toward the *padres* and pleaded for protection.

The *padres*, their long robes blowing around their ankles, took one look at the drove of pigs rampaging in the church, raised their hands in horror, and ordered that the pigs be slaughtered as soon as the butcher could be called.

It turned out that there was a ship waiting in the harbor. The captain heard the commotion in the distance, the shouts of the *padres*, the tearful calls of Don José and his men, and the shrieks and wails of the others around the church, plus the squeals of the pigs. The captain dashed out of his cabin onto the deck and shouted to his crew, "Set the sails! Weigh the anchor!"

Faster than it takes to say, the ship went sailing out of the harbor, its bell ringing loudly to sound a general alarm.

The pigs stopped milling around the church. They pricked up their ears and recurled their tails, and then every one of them went charging toward

the harbor, joyously following the sound of the ship's bell. Panting and snorting, they rushed onto the beach. They paused just long enough to listen again to the ship's clanging bell before they plunged into the surf and began swimming after the vessel.

When last seen, according to a certain sailor whose name is unknown, they were approaching the Hawaiian Islands.

The Great Don José was so crushed by the sight of his pet pigs swimming off without so much as a farewell, he could barely ride back to his ranch. His loyal *caballeros* tried to console him, but it was no use. Grimly, Don José walked off to his flying palm tree, dug up its roots, and climbed aboard. With his tears falling so thickly they created the fog that still sweeps the California coast, he rode off and never was seen again.

giant's wife

The terrible giant had a wife
 Who was almost twelve feet tall.
She slept with her head in the kitchen
 And her feet way out in the hall.

Anonymous

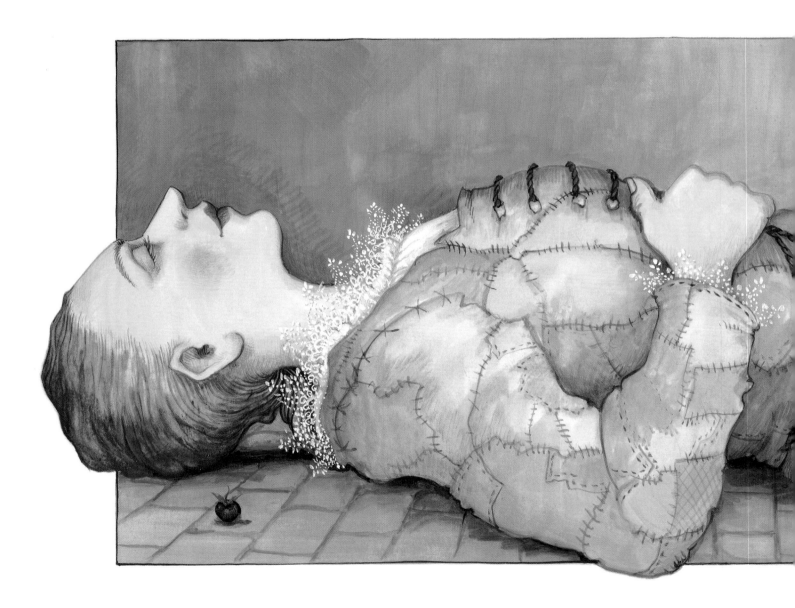

little lella

ITALIAN

PICCINO WAS THE SMALLEST SHEPHERD boy in the valley. It took a long time for Piccino to grow, because he had made a terrible mistake. And this is how it happened.

One day Piccino saw an old woman carrying a basket of apples on her head. The apples were bright and red and huge. Piccino was instantly jealous. "Why should apples grow so big when I'm so puny?" he thought. So he picked up a stone and threw it at the basket, which toppled to the ground.

The old woman picked up a bruised apple. "Wicked boy, tiny boy, you will rue this day. For you will never grow until you find lovely Little Lella of the three singing apples."

4 8

The old woman's curse came true. The years passed, and Piccino grew no taller. Indeed, he grew as thin and pinched as a withering apple.

Finally, Piccino told his mother of the old woman and the apples. "There's no time to lose," she said. "You must find lovely Little Lella."

Piccino started out early the next day, his eyes scanning the orchards, his ears listening for any hint of singing apples. He came to a bridge. A tiny lady sat in half a walnut shell that hung on a thread from one of the supports. Her eyes were closed.

"Lift my eyelids, please, sweet lad. I long so to see the dawn." Piccino lifted her lids, and the lady looked out with joy. "Enough. Thank you," she said. "And in return, pick up the first mossy stone you spy. It will serve you well. Oh, by the way, the singing apples sit in a cage of bells."

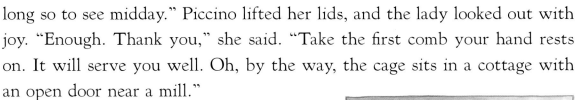

Piccino continued on his way. He came to a second bridge. A second tiny lady sat in half a walnut shell, her eyes closed.

"Lift my eyelids, please, sweet lad. I long so to see midday." Piccino lifted her lids, and the lady looked out with joy. "Enough. Thank you," she said. "Take the first comb your hand rests on. It will serve you well. Oh, by the way, the cage sits in a cottage with an open door near a mill."

Piccino continued on his way. He came to a third bridge. At the edge of the stream a tiny lady stood, filling a gossamer bag with fog. Her eyes were closed.

"Lift my eyelids, please, sweet lad. I long so to see the dusk." Piccino lifted her lids, and the lady looked out with joy.

"Enough. Thank you. Take this bag, fill it with the first pungent breath you smell. It will serve you well." And she gave him the bag. "Oh, by the way, in the cottage sits an old woman. But beware."

Piccino continued on his way. He came to a mill. Nearby stood a cottage with a door wedged open by a mossy stone. Piccino put the stone in his pocket. He entered the dark cottage and saw an old woman sitting by the fire. "Hello, old woman," he said.

The woman said nothing. She was asleep.

Piccino moved closer. In the woman's hair was an ivory comb, smooth as glass, which he slipped into his pocket. Her breath was pungent with fermenting apples. He took out the gossamer bag and filled it with the old woman's breath.

Then Piccino saw a cage with three bright red apples in the center. He picked it up and rushed from the cottage. But as the cage swung from his hand, bells tinkled, for the cage was covered with a thousand singing bells.

Instantly, the old woman awoke. She called a hundred horsemen to chase Piccino and bring back her precious cage. Piccino threw the mossy stone behind

him. It turned into a rocky mountain. All the horses stumbled and fell.

The old woman called two hundred horsemen to chase Piccino and bring back her precious cage. Piccino threw the ivory comb behind him. It turned into an icy pond, slick as glass. All the horses slid and fell.

Then the old woman called three hundred horsemen to chase Piccino and bring back her precious cage. Piccino threw the bag behind him. It opened up, and the old woman's breath turned to fog. All the horses lost their way.

And so Piccino managed to get back to his village. He was hungry after all this time, so he stopped at a well and cut one of the apples in half. Inside the apple he saw a lovely, tiny woman.

"I am Little Lella," she said. "And I'm famished. Would you get me a cake while I wait here?"

While he was away, an old woman came to the well. She spied beautiful Little Lella. "Wretched lass! Here am I, so big and ugly, and there are you, so small and lovely." With one swift slap, she sent Little Lella tumbling down the well.

Piccino returned and searched for Little Lella. But she was nowhere to be found. He returned home brokenhearted.

That night Piccino's mother went to the well and drew up a bucket of water. Lo and behold, a fish swam in the bucket. She brought it home and fried it for Piccino. After dinner she threw the fish bones out the window.

The very next day, a tiny apple sapling grew near the window. It grew so fast and thick that soon the branches blocked all the light from Piccino's home.

Piccino cut down the tree to let in the light and made a pile of firewood.

In the morning he went out to tend the sheep, as usual. When he came home, he saw a girl, no bigger than he, emerge from the woodpile.

"Little Lella, it's you! Where have you been?"

"An old woman pushed me down the well, and a fish ate me. I turned into his bones. When your mother threw the bones out the window, I changed again—into an apple seed. I was the tree that grew outside your window."

"And you are now the tree that grows inside my heart."

So Piccino and Little Lella fell in love. And he grew. And she grew. And they got married and lived happily.

teeny tiny ghost

A teeny, tiny ghost
no bigger than a mouse,
at most,
lived in a great big house.

It's hard to haunt
a great big house
when you're a teeny tiny ghost
no bigger than a mouse,
at most.

He did what he could do.

So every dark and stormy night—
the kind that shakes the house with fright—
if you stood still and listened right,
you'd hear a
teeny
tiny

BOO!

Lilian Moore

JERRY hall

Jerry Hall, he was so small,
A rat could eat him,
Hat and all.

Anonymous

the fairy
cobbler

What do you think I saw to-day
    When I walked forth to take the air?
I saw a little house of hay,
    All in a pasture fair.

And just within the green grass door
    I saw a little cobbler sit:
He sat crossed-legged upon the floor,
    And tapped, tip-tit, tip-tit!

"What are you making there so neat?"
    "Gaiters for glow-worms," he made reply,
"And thistledown slippers for fairy feet,
    And garden boots for a butterfly."

"What do they pay you, my busy mite?"
    "Some bring me honey and some bring dew
And the glow-worms visit me every night
    And light my chamber through."

                             A. Neil Lyons

Wiley and the hairy Man

AFRICAN-AMERICAN

WILEY AND HIS MOTHER LIVED NEAR a swamp. One day Wiley had to go down to the swamp to cut some bamboo, and his mother said to him, "Take your hound dogs with you, or the Hairy Man will get you."

So Wiley took his hound dogs, but when he got to the swamp, his dogs saw a wild pig and ran away. Wiley began to cut some bamboo, but when he looked up, there was the Hairy Man, coming through the trees.

Wiley was scared. So, quick as he could, he climbed up a big bay tree.

The Hairy Man stood at the foot of the tree and called, "Wiley, what are you doing up there?"

Wiley said, "My mother told me to stay away from you."

The Hairy Man picked up Wiley's ax and began to chop down the tree. Suddenly, Wiley heard his hound dogs yelping. "H-E-E-RE, dogs!" he hollered, and his dogs came running. As soon as the Hairy Man saw them, he fled away into the swamp.

When Wiley got home, he told his mother what had happened.

"Well," his mother said, "the next time you see the Hairy Man, say, 'Hello, Hairy Man. I hear you're the best conjure man around here.' He'll say, 'I reckon I am.'

"Then you say, 'I bet you can't change yourself into an alligator.' And he will. Then you say, 'I bet you can't change yourself into a little possum.' And he will. Then you grab him and throw him into his sack. Then you take the sack and throw it into the river."

The next time Wiley had to go to the swamp, he saw the Hairy Man coming at him through the trees, swinging his sack.

"Hairy Man," said Wiley, "I hear you're the best conjure man around here."

"I reckon I am," said the Hairy Man.

Then Wiley said, "I bet you can't change yourself into an alligator."

"Sure I can. That's no trouble at all." And he changed himself into an alligator. So Wiley said, "I bet you can't change yourself into a little possum." The alligator changed itself into a little possum. Wiley grabbed the possum and threw it into the Hairy Man's sack. He tied the sack up tight, threw it into the river, and started back home through the swamp.

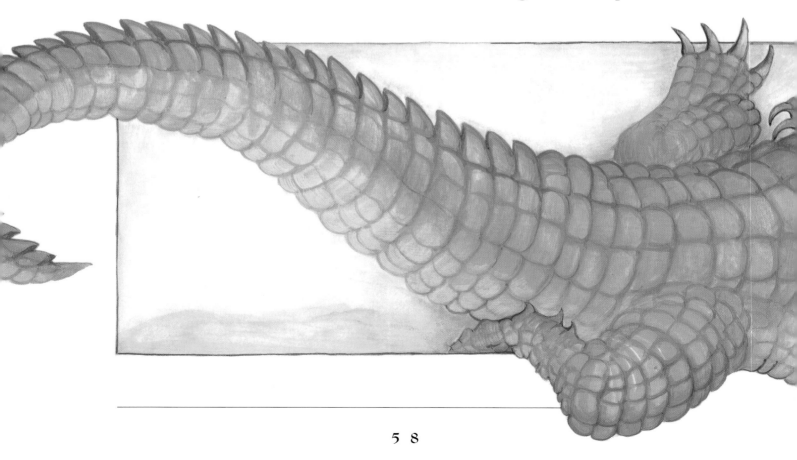

He hadn't gone far when there was the Hairy Man again, so Wiley climbed right up the nearest tree. "How did you get out of the sack?" he called down to the Hairy Man.

"I changed myself into the wind," said the Hairy Man, "and I blew my way out. Now I'm going to wait right down here. You'll get hungry and come down out of that tree."

Wiley thought and thought. He remembered that he had left his hound dogs tied up at home with rope. After a while Wiley said, "Hairy Man, you did some pretty good tricks. But I bet you can't make things disappear."

"Ha! That's what I'm best at. Look at your shirt," said the Hairy Man. Wiley looked down. His shirt was gone! "Oh, that was just a plain old shirt," said Wiley. "But this rope around my pants is magic. I bet you can't make this rope disappear."

The Hairy Man said, "I can make all the rope in this county disappear."

"I bet you can't," said Wiley.

The Hairy Man hollered loud, "All the rope in this county disappear!"

The rope around Wiley's pants was gone. Wiley hollered, "H-E-E-E-RE, dogs!" The dogs came running, and the Hairy Man fled away.

When Wiley got home, he told his mother what had happened. "Well," she said, "you fooled the Hairy Man twice. If we can fool him again, he'll never come back to bother us." Wiley's mother sat down to think.

After a while she said, "Wiley, go down to the pen and bring me back a young pig." She put the piglet in Wiley's bed.

His mother said, "Wiley, now you go up to the loft and hide."

The wind howled and the house shook. Wiley heard footsteps on the roof over his head. The Hairy Man was trying to come down the chimney. When the Hairy Man touched the chimney and found it was hot, he cursed and swore. Then he jumped down and walked right up to the front door. He banged on it and yelled out, "Momma, I've come for your young'un!"

But Wiley's mother called back, "You can't have him, Hairy Man!"

The Hairy Man said, "I'll set your house on fire with lightning if you don't give him to me!"

But Wiley's mother called back, "I have plenty of sweet milk, Hairy Man. The milk will put out your fire."

"I'll dry up your cow," said the Hairy Man. "I'll send a million boll weevils out of the ground to eat your cotton if you don't give up your young'un."

"Hairy Man," said Wiley's mother, "that's mighty mean."

"I'm a mighty mean man," said the Hairy Man.

So Wiley's mother said, "If I give you the young'un, will you go away and never come back?"

"I swear I will," said the Hairy Man.

Wiley's mother opened the door. "He's over in that bed," she said. The Hairy Man walked over to the bed. He snatched the cover back.

"Hey!" he yelled. "There's nothing in this bed but a young pig!"

"I never said which young'un I'd give you," Wiley's mother answered. The Hairy Man stomped his feet. He raged and yelled. He gnashed his teeth. Then he grabbed the piglet and fled away into the swamp.

"The Hairy Man is gone for good," said Wiley's mother. And Wiley and his mother never saw him again.

magic story for falling asleep

When the last giant came out of his cave
and his bones turned into the mountain
and his clothes turned into the flowers,

nothing was left but his tooth
which my dad took home in his trunk
which my granddad carved into a bed

which my mom tucks me into at night
when I dream of the last giant
when I fall asleep on the mountain.

Nancy Willard

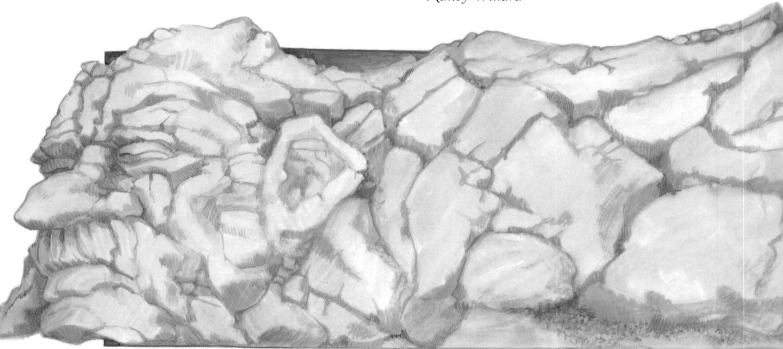

NOTES ON THE STORIES

♦ HOW BIG-MOUTH WRESTLED THE GIANT
This story from the Western European tradition echoes the same motif as two of the most well-known giant tales, "Jack the Giant Killer" and "Jack and the Beanstalk." In these stories the evil giant is vanquished by a young whippersnapper with greater wit. Big-Mouth's personality "flaw" is what saves him in this case, but it also shows that the giant is not the only unsympathetic character in the story.

♦ THE SHOEMAKER AND THE ELVES is one of the best-known Western European folktales. Under the title "The Elves," it was collected by the Brothers Grimm (Grimm #39). Elves, or little folk, are often associated with good luck: a common theme in folk stories is that of elves who come secretly to help worthy humans, not only without asking a reward but sometimes disappearing when their good deeds are recognized.

♦ THREE STRONG WOMEN This story—about a man who prides himself on his strength and is shown up by not one, but three, members of the supposedly weaker sex—is a shorter version of an ancient Japanese tale collected by Claus Stamm. Like American tall tales, it employs exaggeration for comic effect.

♦ ANANSI AND THE PLANTAINS Anansi, the famous African trickster figure, is both spider and tiny man. Stories about him originated in West Africa and were brought to the West Indies by slaves. Like this one, many Anansi tales incorporated the experiences and language of the Africans there. Although Anansi sometimes loses out, usually he wins what he wants for himself through his clever manipulations.

♦ MANAGING MOLLY The word *ogre* was often used interchangeably with *giant*, although today the connotations of the two are quite different. Giants are always physically large, but their brains seldom are, allowing the smaller but brighter humans to outsmart them, as in this tale. The original, longer version of this tale, by English author Juliana Horatia Ewing (1841–1885), was called "The Ogre Courting." Most of her stories appeared in the popular nineteenth-century children's periodical *Aunt Judy's Magazine*.

♦ TEENY-TINY This story was originally collected in Joseph Jacobs's *English Fairy Tales*. It is the best known of a number of variants about a spirit who comes back to claim the part of his body inadvertently exhumed. Some of the fun in telling this tale comes from the repetition of the phrase *teeny-tiny* and from the last line, which brings the story to its startling, funny ending.

♦ LOVESICK LOPEZ was originally recorded in *The California Folklore Quarterly*. The *caballero* Don José Lopez is not as well known as some of his larger-than-life counterparts from other parts of the country—Paul Bunyan, Mike Fink, and Sally Ann Thunder—who have found their way into the literature as folk heroes. This particularly American form of story has its origins in the oral tradition, especially tall talk or exaggerated storytelling. Some tall-tale characters—such as Davy Crockett and Johnny Appleseed (John Chapman)—were actual people, but their exploits or physical prowess or courage were elaborated on as the stories about them were told. Others, however, such as Stormalong and Febold Feboldson, were wholly imaginary.

♦ LITTLE LELLA *Lella* is a diminutive of the Italian name *Elena*. World folklore is full of human characters, both male and female, who are tiny; Thumbelina and Little Thumbkin, from the Western European tradition, and Little Peachling, from Japan, are examples. This story shares common motifs with many other tales: three labors or trials facing a protagonist, a fruit that is cut open to reveal a tiny person inside, and a person reforming herself from discarded bones. For other stories from Italy, see *Italian Tales* and *Italian Fables*, collected by Italo Calvino, the noted Italian writer and anthologist.

♦ WILEY AND THE HAIRY MAN This African-American story is based on an Alabama folktale recorded by Donnell Van de Voort for the Federal Writers' Project of the Works Progress Administration. The Hairy Man is part African ogre with long matted hair and part new-world conjure man, a kind of hoodoo doctor who could work magic with the use of charms or spells.

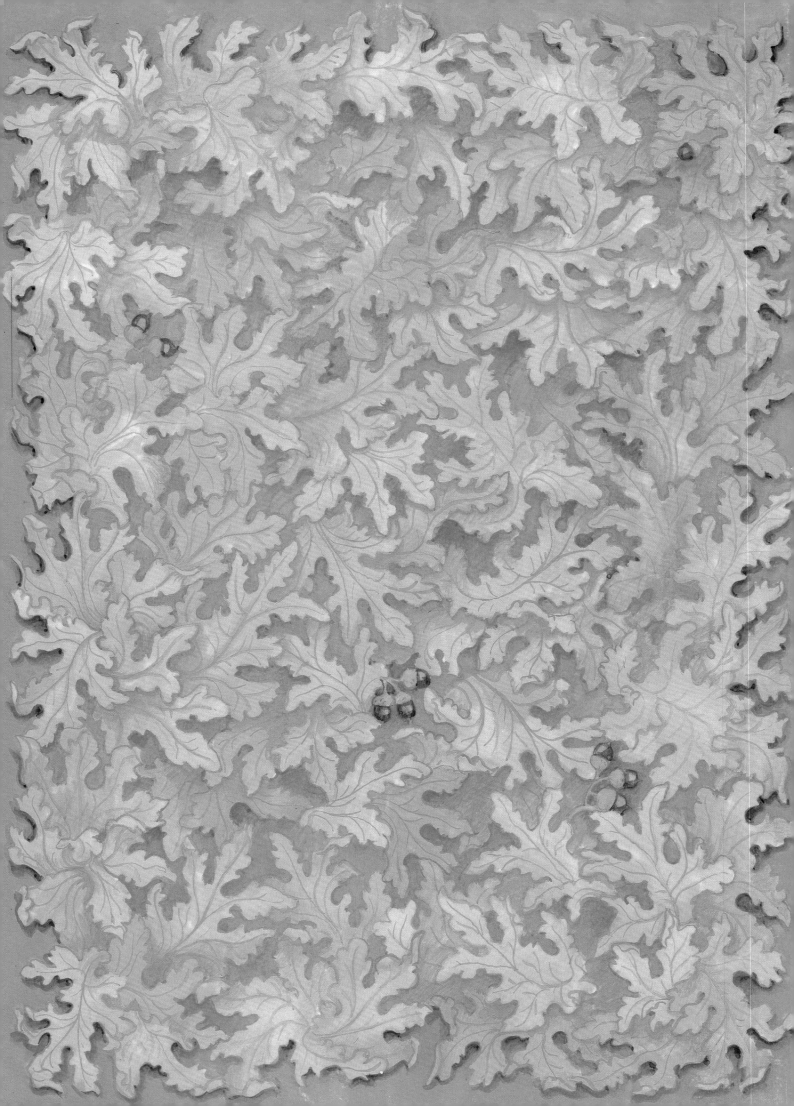